TINY TUTU
Is All Mixed Up

By Cassidy Rae Duborg

Illustrated by Deborah Partington

Published by Orange Hat Publishing 2021
ISBN 9781645383314

Copyrighted © 2021 by Cassidy Rae Duborg
All Rights Reserved
Tiny Tutu Is All Mixed Up
Written by Cassidy Rae Duborg
Illustrated by Deborah Partington

This publication and all contents within may not be reproduced or transmitted in any part or in its entirety without the written permission of the author.

www.orangehatpublishing.com

To my family, for your unwavering love
and support – thank you.

Hi there! My name is Petunia, but all my friends call me Tiny Tutu. I'm a pug dog, just like the rest of my family.

Daddy is a black pug, Mommy is a fawn pug, and my sister, Winifred, is a fawn pug. She likes to be called Winnie for short! We always go to the park and play together. My family is the best!

"Petunia, it's time for your first day of school!"
Mom yells up the stairs.

I run the brush through my fur as fast as I can, then bound down the stairs - I don't want to be late on my first day!

I grab my backpack, then Mommy and I are out the door. We trot down our long driveway to the mailbox as the big, yellow school bus putt-putt-putts down the street.

"Have a great first day of school, Petunia!" Mommy says as the school bus comes to a halt in front of us.

The doors slowly pull open, and the bus driver says, "Hi, I'm Mr. Jones. You must be Petunia!"

I climb the stairs all the way to the top, then look down the aisles filled with puppies. There are all different breeds, even some I've never seen before!

"You can sit right over there, Tiny Tutu," Mr. Jones says. I make my way through the aisle and sit down as the bus starts to move.

Bumping and thumping down the road,
I look around at all the new faces.
"Hi, I'm Petunia, but you can call me Tiny Tutu,"
I say to the girl sitting across from me.

"Hi, I'm Rose."

"I'm Lucky!" barks the boy next to Rose, popping out of his seat.

"It's nice to meet you!" I respond.

"I'm a Labrador, and Rose here is a Rottweiler. What are you?" asks Lucky.

"I'm a pug!" I say proudly, showing him my curly tail and wrinkly face.

"But you don't look like a pug – you have black and grey and white spots all over. Pugs have to be solid black or fawn. You're not any of those! So how are you a real pug?" Lucky criticizes.

I don't know what Lucky means. My mommy and daddy and sister are pugs, so that makes me a pug, right?

"I'm a pug," I say again, with a little less confidence.

Lucky looks me up and down, then says, "There's no way you're a real pug. You're all mixed up. Rose and I only talk to real dogs."

"Oh," I say. Then I turn to look out the window with tears in my eyes. It really hurts my feelings that Lucky thinks I'm not a real dog.

Finally, we pull up to school, and it's GIANT! So many windows, doors, and other students! I follow the other dogs off the bus and into the classroom.

"Welcome, students! Please find your desks and take a seat," the teacher announces from the front of the room.
"I'm Miss Perry. Welcome to class!"

I wander around until I find a desk with my name on it and sit down. Once all the students are at their desks, Miss Perry asks us to introduce ourselves as well as our breed.

"I'll start!" Miss Perry says. "My name is Miss Perry, and I'm a poodle."

We go around the room as each student barks their name and breed. Finally, it's my turn. "My name is Petunia, and I'm a pug," I say hesitantly.

After all the puppies introduce themselves, we spend the rest of the day playing games, learning about numbers, and running around chasing our tails at recess!

Eventually, the bell rings and it's time to go home.

I follow the students out the door, into the hall, and back onto the bus. I don't talk to anyone because I'm still thinking about what Lucky said. What does he mean I'm all mixed up? And why can't I be a real pug with spots?

"Tiny Tutu, this is your stop!" Mr. Jones barks.

"Thanks, Mr. Jones!" I say and scamper off the bus.

I see Mommy right away, waiting for me at the end of the driveway. I run up to her and give her a BIG hug. "How was your day, sweetie?" she asks.

"I'm all mixed up," I say, feeling a little defeated.

"Now what in the world does that mean?" asks Mommy as we trot back to the house.

Once inside, I sit down at the kitchen table right next to Daddy. He nuzzles my nose, "You made it through your first day of school! How did it go, Tiny?"

I look down at the table and mumble, "Fine."

Daddy pauses and then asks, "Now, Tiny Tutu, what happened? Your first day of school should be more than fine."

I look at Daddy, then at Mommy, and blurt out, "Lucky says I don't look like a real pug because I'm not black or fawn. He says I'm all mixed up with my black, white, and grey spots. He won't even talk to me!"

Mommy comes over and pulls me in close. "Petunia, it doesn't matter what you look like on the outside. It only matters that you carry kindness inside your heart."

Then Daddy says, "Not everyone looks the same, and that's what makes each dog so special! I'm a black pug, Mommy is a fawn pug, and that's how we made you – a beautiful merle pug."

"What's a merle pug?" I ask.

"The word 'merle' describes what your fur looks like. You have extraordinary black, white, and grey spots! They make you special and no less of a pug," Daddy says.

Mommy chimes in, "You should be friends with dogs because they are kind, smart, and helpful – not because of what they look like. And that's why other dogs should be friends with you, too!"

"So yes, you are a little mixed up," Daddy says, "but in the best way possible! Always remember that."

"Thanks, Mommy! Thanks, Daddy!" I say as I squeeze them both tight, feeling much better.

The next morning, Mommy and I walk to the bus stop, and she asks, "How are you feeling today, Tiny?"

"All mixed up, but in just the right way!" I bark right back.

Mr. Jones pulls up the big, yellow school bus, and I hop on. "Good morning, Mr. Jones!"

"Good morning, Tiny Tutu!"

I find my seat and plop down. Lucky and Rose are sitting across from me, just like yesterday.

Lucky looks at me and says, "Tiny Tutu, the pretend pug," and sticks his tongue out.

I look back at Lucky and say, "You're not being a very kind friend. I'm a merle pug, which means I have these beautiful black, white, and grey spots. It doesn't matter what I look like on the outside, because I am a kind friend on the inside."

"She's right," woofs Rose. "Tiny Tutu, can I be your friend?"

"You sure can!" I say. "Do you want to sit together?"

"Sure!" answers Rose as she scoots across the aisle.

She compliments my spots and I pet her soft, short fur. Rose and I talk all the way to school, becoming fast friends.

We're each unique in our own way, and that's what makes us special! Being a mixed-up merle pug is pretty great after all.

CPSIA information can be obtained
at www.ICGtesting.com
Printed in the USA
BVHW021626301121
622774BV00003B/172